COLA POWER

For Rowan Class
at Whitchurch School

ORCHARD BOOKS
338 Euston Road, London NW1 3BH
Orchard Books Australia
Level 17/207 Kent Street, Sydney, NSW 2000

First published in 2010
First paperback publication in 2011

ISBN 978 1 40830 256 9 (hardback)
ISBN 978 1 40830 264 4 (paperback)

Text and illustrations © Shoo Rayner 2010

The right of Shoo Rayner to be identified as the author and
illustrator of this work has been asserted by him in accordance
with the Copyright, Designs and Patents Act, 1988.

A CIP catalogue record for this book is available
from the British Library.

1 3 5 7 9 10 8 6 4 2 (hardback)
1 3 5 7 9 10 8 6 4 2 (paperback)

Printed in Great Britain

Orchard Books is a division of Hachette Children's Books,
an Hachette UK company.

COLA POWER

SHOO RAYNER

ORCHARD BOOKS

CHAPTER ONE

"Ow!" Something sharp and pointy bounced off Axel Storm's head and plopped into the guitar-shaped swimming pool next to him.

Axel groaned. "What was that? I'd nearly finished this level. Now I'll have to start all over again!" Axel was at Master Level on *Death Flight 3000* and was very close to Genius Status.

He put down his games controller and peered into the pool. A soggy paper aeroplane bobbed limply on the waves. Axel fished it out. Water dripped from its bent nose.

"Where on earth did this come from?" Axel wondered.

Axel looked around the pool area and across the velvet-green tennis courts beyond. The multi-million pound estate where he lived lay quiet and serene in the sunshine.

"That'll be from your Uncle Telford," Axel's dad said, as he floated past on an inflatable desert island. "He always sends messages like that. He's barmy about aeroplanes."

Axel unfolded the plane. Watery
letters trickled across the soggy paper.

42 Runway Road

Little Handley

A380 737

Dear Axel,

I need the help of a young and
enthusiastic assistant, with
computer game experience, for a
very important, very secret project
I'm working on.

  Come over next week. I hope
you're not afraid of heights!

Uncle Telford

"A secret project? That sounds brilliant!" Axel said. "Can I go, Dad?"

Dad picked a can of Power Cola out of an inflatable ice box, snapped it open and downed it in one enormous glug.

"Sorry, son, the answer's no. Your uncles just can't be trusted. You always end up having dangerous adventures with them! Anyway, we're off on tour next week." He paused to let out a thunderous burp.

"Oh, Dad!" Axel complained. "That's gross!"

Dad reached for another can and smiled. "Son, when you are as famous as I am, you can burp all you like."

Axel's Mum and Dad were rock stars. Their band, Stormy Skies, had recorded twenty-two platinum-selling hits in eighty-three different countries around the world. They spent most of their lives travelling, performing concerts and meeting their millions of fans.

The Storm family were rich – really, really rich. But even though they were richer than you can ever imagine being rich, they still tried to live normal lives…sort of.

For instance, they only had one massive mansion in each of the ten countries they lived in…

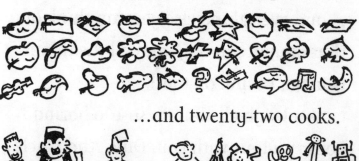

…only thirty luxury swimming pools…

…and twenty-two cooks.

Not to mention…

…only ten super cars…

…eight private jets…

…a helicopter…

…and everything else you can think of that money can buy (and all the things you can't think of, too!).

Axel sighed. "But it's so-o-o boring going on tour with you, Dad. And Uncle Telford is a brilliant inventor. It will probably be really *educational*."

Axel knew his parents couldn't say
no if he used the word "educational".
It worked nearly every time.

Axel's mum rolled over on her
sunbed, making sure her suntan was
nice and even.

She smiled her dazzling smile.
"Maybe we should let him go, Thrust?
Uncle Telford can keep Axel away from
Archie Flash, that horrid photographer
who's always trying to get his picture for
Celebrity Gossip Magazine."

Axel smiled sweetly at his dad,
waiting for him to give in.

"Oh, OK!" Dad peered over the top of
his mirrored sunglasses. "You can go!"

"Yes!" Axel punched the air.
"Thanks, Dad."

CHAPTER TWO

A week later, the Stormy Skies tour bus arrived in Runway Road.

There wasn't a house where number forty-two should have been. Instead, an old propeller aeroplane was parked at the end of the path. The number "42" was painted on the door!

"Cool…" Axel whispered, ringing the bell.

A muffled voice came from inside. "Hello?"

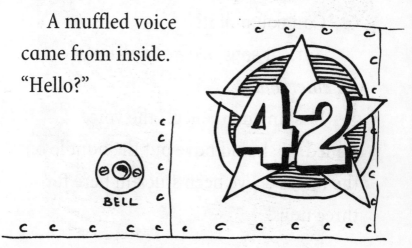

BELL

Axel raised his voice, "Is that you, Uncle Telford?"

"Who's there?"

"It's Axel."

"Can you see a red handle that says, *Do not pull unless in an emergency!*?"

"Yes!"

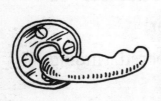 

"Can you pull it?"

"But…it says, *Do not pull unless in an emergency!*"

"It is an emergency!" the voice fumed. "I should have put the handle on the inside – I've been stuck in here for three days!"

Axel pulled the emergency handle. The door opened with a loud *pish!*

Uncle Telford poked his head out and smiled. The top pocket of his overalls bristled with pens and rulers and packets of mints. An aeroplane design was woven on the front of his greasy cap.

"Axel!" Uncle Telford ruffled Axel's hair. "Haven't you grown?"

Axel smiled politely. Why did grown-ups always say that?

"Telford!" Dad yelled.

"Storm!" Uncle Telford yelled back.

The two brothers hugged as if they hadn't seen each other for years.

"Look after Axel," Dad said, slapping his brother on the back.

"And don't let any photographers get near him!" Mum ordered.

Mum and Dad leapt back on their bus. "We love you, Axel!" they shouted. "See you soon! Be good, and don't go having any of your adventures!"

Uncle Telford gave Axel a mischievous smile. Axel couldn't wait to find out about his uncle's secret project and how he could help...

CHAPTER THREE

"Is this your plane?" Axel asked.

"Certainly is," Uncle Telford smiled. "It's a Dakota DC3. I've been doing her up. Want to come in?"

In the doorway, Axel stopped and stared. "This is so cool!" he cooed.

The floor was covered in rubber tiles. Rows of little cupboards lined the walls and light flooded in from a glass roof.

"Do you live here?" Axel asked.

"Certainly do," said Uncle Telford. "Your room's in the bomb bay."

"Brilliant!" said Axel. "So – what do you need help with?"

"All in good time," said Uncle Telford with a wink. "All in good time. First, we have to test your flying skills…"

Flying skills? Axel thought. *What is this secret project…?*

"Any good at computer games?"
Uncle Telford asked. He opened a
laptop and swung it round so Axel
could see.

"Well, I've just been awarded
Genius Status on *Death Flight 3000*!"
Axel enthused.

"This is a state-of-the-art flight
simulator game," Uncle Telford
explained. "It's more difficult than any
other. Let's see if you can handle it."

Uncle Telford gave Axel a controller and showed him how to play. "Wait till your power is fully charged, then go for take off."

Axel read the screen and checked the controls. "No problem," he said confidently.

Axel piloted the virtual plane like a professional. "Woohoo! This game is awesome. It's so fast!"

"OK, that's good," Uncle Telford smiled. "Now, see if you can fly through the obstacle course."

On the screen, Axel flew the plane under bridges…

…in between buildings…

…and through rocky canyons.

Uncle Telford clapped his hands. "Excellent! Now, bring it in to land and press the red turbo-landing button at the last moment."

"Woooargh! That's amazing," Axel squealed, as he expertly brought the plane into a vertical landing. "I got three thousand points – is that good?"

Uncle Telford grinned and nodded. "You qualify as a test pilot!"

Axel's eyebrows shot up. "Test pilot for what?"

"Come out to the shed and see!" said Uncle Telford. His eyes twinkled with excitement.

CHAPTER FOUR

Axel followed his uncle to the bottom of
the garden. A door-sized hole had been
cut into a huge fir-tree hedge.

"I don't believe it!" Axel gasped,
when he saw what was on the other
side. The enormous body of a jumbo jet
aeroplane filled the field beyond.

"That's my inventing shed," Uncle
Telford announced proudly.

"It's gigantic!" Axel was impressed.

"It took three giant cranes to hoist
it over the hedge!" Uncle Telford
explained.

Inside the huge plane were workbenches covered in tools, chemistry experiments and computer screens that glowed with ever-changing rows of shapes and numbers.

"Aeroplanes have always been my passion," said Uncle Telford. "But this is my special, secret project!"

He tugged a dust sheet with a magician's flourish, revealing a small, but perfectly formed, aeroplane.

"I call it the Green Dart," he whispered.

"It's made entirely from recycled materials," Uncle Telford continued. "I'm taking it to the Power Cola Flying Competition tomorrow. Inventors from all around the world will be showing off their ideas for pollution-free flight."

"The Power Cola Flying Competition? Wow!" Uncle Telford had got Axel's attention. "Isn't that Joe McCola's new big idea?"

Everyone knew about Joe McCola. He was a very powerful businessman and the boss of the Power Cola Corporation. His beautiful girlfriends and mad publicity stunts got him into the papers all the time, but he was also famous for helping inventors turn their ideas into successful products.

"That's right!" said Uncle Telford. "It's a really important day for me. If I win, Joe McCola will help me make full-sized versions of the Green Dart, so that one day everyone can own one. No one will ever need cars again!"

"Wow…" Axel ran his fingers over the plane's sleek surface. "It feels…squeaky." Axel was surprised. "Like…it's almost alive."

"It is!" Uncle Telford explained. "It's covered in plant cells. That's why it's green! The plant cells make energy from sunshine through a special process. The energy powers the internal thrust system."

"Wow!" Axel was amazed. "And what do you want me to do?" he asked.

"I want you to fly it!" Uncle Telford raised his eyebrows, waiting for Axel's reaction.

Axel's jaw dropped. "B-b-but!" he stammered. "You mean you think I could fly the Green Dart?"

Uncle Telford sunk his hands into the pockets of his white lab coat.

"I certainly do. The Green Dart is my life's work. If it doesn't win the competition tomorrow, it will all have been for nothing. You've qualified as a test pilot, and it's just your size."

"C-o-o-ol!" Axel swooned. "Mum and Dad will go crazy when they find out!"

CHAPTER FIVE

Outside, Uncle Telford showed Axel how everything worked.

"Are they bombs?" Axel pointed to the black tanks under the wings.

"They're the landing retro-boosters," explained Uncle Telford.

"They look like Power Cola bottles!"

"They are!" Uncle Telford laughed. "I added them to impress Joe McCola."

Uncle Telford placed a new bottle on the floor and unscrewed the top. He took three mints from a packet in his top pocket and dropped them into the cola.

"Watch this!" he giggled.

The cola bottle turned white and began to shake. Suddenly, a streaming fountain of fizzy cola burst up into the air like a volcanic geyser!

"That's what happens when you press the red turbo-landing button!" Uncle Taylor giggled. "The retro thrust is carbon-neutral and recyclable too!"

Axel climbed into the plane's cockpit and got the feel of the controls.

"It's a nice, sunny day. The plant cells have been making energy, so there's lots of take-off power," Uncle Telford explained. "Why don't you take it for a spin? Use the path as your runway. Good luck!"

Axel put his helmet on. "What happens if the sun stops shining?"

"Hmmm!" Uncle Telford looked a bit embarrassed. "Er…that won't be a problem when I make the full-sized version," he mumbled. "Hopefully…"

The controls were just like the computer game – but this was real!

The engine reached full thrust. Axel felt the plane straining to go…

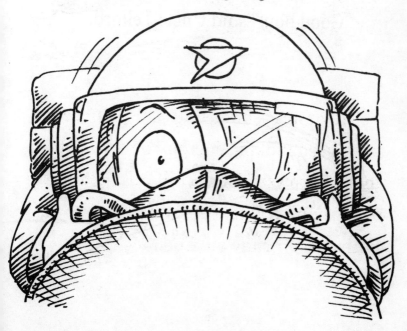

He released the brakes and the Green Dart tore down the path.

"I'm going to hit the hedge!" he yelled.

"Pull up now!" Uncle Telford's voice called in Axel's built-in radio headset.

Axel pulled back hard on the thrust controller. The Green Dart lifted off the ground. The wheels just scraped the top of the hedge.

"Good boy!" said Uncle Telford.

"This is so cool, Uncle Telford," Axel called into his microphone. "I'm really flying!"

The sky was blue, the sun was shining and Axel wanted to stay up above the world for ever. He felt as free as a bird – no Mum and Dad to nag him, no magazine photographers trying to sneak pictures of him – just blue sky and fluffy white clouds.

Eventually, Axel let the plane drift
down towards the ground. At the
last moment, he stabbed the red
turbo-landing button.

Cola bubbles filled the air as he made
a perfect landing right on the spot he
was aiming for.

Uncle Telford danced up and down
in excitement. "Brilliant!" he trilled.
"We'll show that Joe McCola tomorrow.
We're sure to win!"

CHAPTER SIX

The next day, Axel and Uncle Telford arrived early at the Power Cola Flying Competition.

Axel could tell Uncle Telford was nervous. This was the biggest day of his life!

Axel spotted Joe McCola right at the front of the VIP stand. He was surrounded by experts who were helping him look for brilliant new inventions – and to choose the winner of the competition.

These were the people Axel needed to impress!

In another stand, photographers from technology magazines had come to take pictures of all the new inventions.

No gossip magazines here! Axel sighed with relief.

"It's our turn at four o'clock," Uncle Telford explained. "Take off in front of the VIP stand, then fly as low and as close as you can to show them what the Green Dart can do. It's a sunny day so there should be plenty of power for the thrusters."

All day long, Uncle Telford made
comments as his rivals' strange
machines took to the air.

"Too smoky…

…too heavy…

…too ugly…

…too loud!"
he muttered.

In no time at all, it was their turn. At quarter to four, Axel climbed into the pilot's seat and ran through his final checks.

As Uncle Telford pushed the plane onto the runway, Axel felt butterflies in his stomach. He was nervous, but he knew he had to help Uncle Telford achieve his life's dream.

Just then, the afternoon sun sank
behind the VIP stand. A dark shadow
fell across the Green Dart.

Axel pressed the start button.
Nothing happened. He pressed it again.
Still nothing happened.

"Uncle Telford?" Axel hissed into his
microphone. "It's not working."

"You're in the shade," Uncle Telford groaned. "The system needs full power for take-off. We need bright light or we're done for. All my hard work wasted – and no one will ever take me seriously again!"

In the VIP stand, Axel saw Joe McCola stand up. He looked like he thought it was a good time to go and visit the VIP toilets.

Then a voice yelled out from a group of photographers. "Hey! Forget the plane! That's Axel Storm in the flying seat!"

Axel's heart sank. It was Archie Flash from *Celebrity Gossip Magazine*! He was probably there to photograph Joe McCola and his latest girlfriend. But he had spotted Axel sitting in the seat of the Green Dart!

Thirty-two photographers burst out of their stand and ran across the tarmac. A picture of Axel Storm flying a plane would definitely be front-page news in tomorrow's paper.

The camera flashes popped away like a firework display. Axel sank deep into the cockpit. There was nowhere to hide. Mum and Dad were going to kill him!

Suddenly, a loud beep told him the thrusters were zooming up to full power.

"The camera flashes are providing the power!" he whooped into his microphone.

"Brilliant!" Uncle Telford cheered. "You're clear for take off!"

Axel pulled the controller towards
him and the thrusters began to roar
behind his seat. The Green Dart rolled
along the runway, picking up speed.

The crowd of photographers parted
to let him through.

Axel pulled the plane out of the shadow and up into the brilliant sunshine.

"Full power!" he cheered, as he banked tightly and waved to the people in the control tower.

Putting the Green Dart into a steep climb, Axel flipped it over into a perfect loop-the-loop. The crowd *ooh*-ed and *aah*-ed below.

Roaring past the VIP stand, Axel rolled the plane into a series of spins. Joe McCola was open-mouthed in amazement.

Axel showed off everything that the amazing plane could do. He flew the Green Dart fast...

...and he flew it slow.

He flew between aircraft hangars
and under Power Cola banners…

…he flew sideways and upside down…

…and he rolled through the air
like a corkscrew.

Joe McCola and all the experts were on their feet, cheering wildly. The demonstration was a huge success!

"Bring her in!" Uncle Telford's voice crackled on the headset.

Axel looked for the best landing place. The photographers were waiting for him in front of the VIP stand.

A smile spread across his face. Axel had been followed by photographers from the day he was born. It was always good to get his own back.

He swooped into landing mode over the knot of photographers and pressed the turbo-landing button.

With a loud pop, the cola bottle tops blew off and clouds of brown bubbles exploded from the Green Dart's wings, drenching the photographers in sweet, sticky Power Cola.

"Sorreee!" Axel called, as he climbed out of the plane.

Archie Flash was soaked to the skin, but he didn't mind. He'd got his picture!

Joe McCola marched across the tarmac and ruffled Axel's hair. "That was great flying, son," he bellowed.

Joe shook Uncle Telford's hand. "Congratulations, sir," he boomed. "With my help and your plane, Cola Power is going to save the human race from ecological disaster!"

"Does that mean we've won the competition?" Axel asked excitedly.

"Sure does," Joe McCola thundered. "Soon, everyone will have a plane like this. No one will ever need to drive a car again."

Uncle Telford grinned and gave Axel a high-five.

"Smile for the camera!" Archie Flash beamed.

CHAPTER SEVEN

"I don't know how you do it," Axel's
dad moaned. The band's tour was
over and they were driving home in
the tour bus. The table was covered
in newspapers.

"It's all Telford's fault," Mum sighed.
"He was supposed to keep you away
from photographers, and here you are
on the front page of every newspaper
in the land!"

"Stormy Skies only get a small picture on page nineteen," Dad grumbled. "You're more famous than we are!"

Mum gave Axel a concerned look. "We do so want you to grow up like a normal boy, Axel."

Axel shrugged his shoulders and smiled as he read about his latest adventure.

Uncle Telford had let him keep the Green Dart. It would be waiting for him when he got back home. *Death Flight 3000* wouldn't seem so exciting any more.

"Joe McCola says that soon everyone will have a plane like the Green Dart," Axel said. "When that day comes, I'll be normal, just like everyone else!"

CELEBRITY
GOSSIP
MAGAZINE

Celebrity kid **AXEL STORM** wowed the Power Cola Flying Competition yesterday, when he demonstrated his Uncle Telford's latest invention, the Green Dart.

JOE McCOLA will be putting the amazing new plane into mass production.

Joe McCola said,

"COLA POWER IS THE FUTURE!"

Axel was not available for comment. His Uncle Telford said, "That boy can really fly!"

By ace reporter, Archie Flash.

SHOO RAYNER

ALL PRICED AT £3.99

Orchard Books are available from all good bookshops,
or can be ordered from our website: www.orchardbooks.co.uk,
or telephone 01235 827702, or fax 01235 827703.